After

Diana Denisse

A JOLLY EVER AFTER

DIANA DENISSE

Copyright © 2024 by Diana Denisse

All rights reserved.

No part of this book may be reproduced in any form or by any electronic or mechanical means, including information storage and retrieval systems, without written permission from the author, except for the use of brief quotations in a book review.

ISBN: 979-8-9909424-3-1

To my happy ever after, Daniel.

Contents

Chapter 1	1
Chapter 2	9
Chapter 3	17
Chapter 4	26
Chapter 5	33
Chapter 6	40
Chapter 7	45
Chapter 8	51
Chapter 9	55
Acknowledgments	61
About The Author	63

Chapter One

Whatever the world might bring at our feet, we will walk through it together. I sigh and close the book. Happily ever afters are so final and beautiful in books. I know nothing about them, but a girl can dream.

The woman sitting next to me on the plane reads out loud the title of my novel. "Is it good?" she asks.

I find it rude when strangers force me into small talk, mostly when I'm stuck somewhere. This is the natural way I should make friends, but I hate it. I'm not ready. My social interactions need to be planned by me. I like to attend outings like anyone else, but on my terms. But as I sit waiting for us to deplane, I've no choice but to take part.

"Magic, love and battle. What's there not to love?" I ask and hand her the book so she can read the back.

I'm hoping she'd take a minute looking at it, giving me enough time to prepare my small talk topics, but no luck. She hardly even glances at it.

"The author's name sounds familiar," the woman says.

I shrug because I don't know where it could be from. I picked up the book in a small indie bookstore months ago.

This morning I grabbed it in a wimp while leaving for the flight. I didn't expect to finish the whole thing in one sitting.

"Do you live here or are you visiting?" the woman asks me.

"I used to live here for a couple of years, but I'm only here visiting a friend now," I say.

I love Maine and I loved my time here, but I'm a drifter. The time I spend on planes surpasses the time I spend in one place. I consider myself a modern form of nomad.

"What do you do?" The woman follows up.

The question is typical of two strangers' first meeting.

"I'm a project manager organizing summer camps for a tech curriculum company."

The puzzling scrunch of her brows is common. People often think that since the programs I organize are for summer only, then my company wouldn't need me the rest of the year, but we serve over thirty schools. That's contracts, training and setting up our curriculum in places all over the country. I stay plenty busy, but I'd be lying if I didn't say that the calm work flow wasn't a big reason I love my job.

"How about yourself?" I clear my throat and turn the conversation to her. "Here for business or pleasure?"

By the time she finishes telling me all her vacation plans, it's time to grab my carry-on and deboard the plane.

I spot Cathy across the street as soon as I exit the airport. She's wearing a red oversize coat that makes her look stylish and cozy. I can see the moment she sees me because we both jump in excitement and run towards one another.

"Ahh, I missed you and missed the Maine air," I say to Cathy.

"You hated Maine about a year ago. That's why you ended your lease and took off."

I roll my eyes. Leave it to Cathy to not let me get away with anything. I didn't exactly hate Maine or Maples, the small town we lived in, when I decided not to renew my lease. Instead, I was seeking my next stop. That's what I do. I'm a professional drifter. Due to my job being online, I can do it from anywhere. I only landed in Maine after some beautiful photos of the town had me buying a one-way plane ticket. Then I hit gold by finding a best friend.

"Let me help you with that." She takes my backpack and puts it inside the car. "Are you carrying the world's problems in this thing?"

"Only what I'll need to invade your home for a month. Lead the way." I gesture for her to get moving.

She looks so beautiful with her short black hair. It gives her a pin doll look. She gives me a side hug and I climb into the car. The airport is about an hour away from town. The conversation doesn't seem to stop despite us having spoken on a weekly basis since I left. This is why I think of Cathy as my best friend.

"Where's your new spot?" I ask while looking around, trying to see if anything changed since I was last here. "Nothing really changes here, huh?"

"Nope," she says and fusses over the heating button on the car that doesn't seem to work. "I just moved a couple of blocks away. I'm now across Prosper Park."

"No way!" I jump in place. "Thank you, aunt Clara!"

"May she rest in peace," Cathy says and does a cross across her face.

I follow suit, not trying to anger any aunty in the afterlife.

"Admit it, you hit gold with your aunt's apartment." I

push my friend's shoulder. "Three rooms and two bathrooms."

Who would have thought that aunty would leave her paid off apartment to Cathy? I met the woman once and didn't think she liked Cathy much, to be honest.

"And a studio with enormous windows." Cathy loses all pretense of being unaffected. "I do have a neighbor who's giving me a hard time."

"How so?" I ask.

I would have never felt comfortable enough to come and stay over a month with Cathy if her living situation was the same as when I last lived with her. We once shared a unit with four other girls. Three to a bathroom. While not the worst, the living situation was crowded.

"Just a total asshole, you'll see." She gestures forward. "Do you see the green building ahead?"

"Is that it?" I squeal again. "Let's go."

We find parking in a reserve spot and round the corner for the building's entrance. I use the energy reserve I have left to power walk towards the front. My mission is to cross the space between me and that beautiful green brick building as fast as possible.

"Slow down," Cathy yells behind me. "I can't feel my feet anymore."

I look down at her feet and see she's wearing six-inch stilettos. No sympathy from me, but I wait for her at the doorway. It gives me just enough time to take it all in. There are flowerpots on the windows and none of the paint looks to be peeling off.

"It can't get better than this," I say as she finally reaches my side.

"Oh, you wait." She gives me a smirk that tells me it gets better and I'm about to find out.

"An elevator!" I whisper-shout.

Cathy's grin is big. "I'm so glad I waited this long to tell you. That look on your face made the wait worth it."

We walk into the elevator, but before the doors can close, a man in his thirties walks inside. My friend's smile drops instantly at the sight of the tall, slim man.

"Good morning Cathy," the man says without looking her way, but my friend doesn't answer. Undisturbed by the lack of manners, he turns in my direction. "Good morning."

"Good morning," I say, completely at a loss until I remember what she said on the way here about a neighbor.

The elevator pins again and the door opens. The man steps out on the same floor as us and walks down the hall. Cathy follows in the same direction, but at a much slower pace.

He unlocks the last door in the hall, but before going in, he glances our way and waves. Once he shuts his door, Cathy rushes to her door and fumbles with the keys to get it open.

"Wait a minute," I say as she shuts the door behind us.

"Don't," Cathy warns. She moves straight to the back hallway and opens a door. "This is your room. The bathroom in the hallway is all yours."

I don't move from the front door. Her steps are hurried and for someone who was nearly limping outside the building, she surely has some speed on her step now.

"That's the neighbor giving you a hard time?"

"What, Rosa?" she asks, rolling her eyes and avoiding eye contact.

A smile spreads across my face wide enough to scare. My friend is slowly turning a light shade of cherry.

"Let's just say your neighbor is welcome to give me a hard time."

The speed in which she tosses my bag at my head is admirable. I catch it before it makes contact, but I can hear my items tossing inside.

"I'm kidding. He's totally not my type."

I refrain from pointing out that he's totally hers. I head to my room and kiss her cheek on the way as a thank you and apology for making her mad not even five minutes into my invasion of her space.

"I'll shower and change, then meet you here," I say as I look for fresh clothes in my bag.

"Don't hurry," she says in a dead tone and leaves me.

After a quick shower, I put on my Christmas pajamas. This is the first time I'll be wearing them this year, and it feels like it truly sets the beginning of the season. It's been two days since thanksgiving and I'm proud I at least waited this long.

The smell of Abuelita chocolate is all over the apartment when I step out of my bedroom. A couple of years back, I showed Cathy how adding vanilla and cinnamon sticks to the milk while it boils, is a game changer. From the incredible smell, I can see that my lesson stuck.

"Is that what I think it is?" I ask, walking into the kitchen. I pause just one step inside the room and look around. "Cathy, this place is crazy beautiful."

The photos she sent me don't do this place justice. Big windows and crown moulding all around. The space was clearly well-maintained.

"I figured we can have some hot chocolate with the movie." She hands me a steaming mug. "It might be drinkable when we're done with dinner."

I blow on the rim of my cup and watch the swirls fly and dissipate into the air.

"What's your plan for your stay in town?" Cathy asks as she serves dinner.

"I have a list of things I want to do. A Christmas wish list with a very ambitious finale."

"Really?" She arches her brow.

"What?" I ask.

I feel judgment coming.

"Nothing." She shrugs. "I mean, you lived here before and didn't care to do more than join that cult."

I roll my eyes. "I'll also be joining my bingo club again."

"The fact that our town has a bingo club is ridiculous," she says, exasperated.

My time with the seasoned ladies at bingo was amazing. Who knew I could have so much in common with them? They're actually what inspired the last item on my list. Each of them has influenced a town holiday tradition in the past. I find that cool. You essentially have a hand at starting something people will do and enjoy for years to come. If I'm lucky, this tradition will outlive me. I just have to figure out what it is.

"You've nothing to say about the last item on the list?" I wiggle my brows.

Cathy looks again, then bursts into laughter. "You've been hanging out too much with those old ladies."

I shriek back. "You've something bad to say about Patty and Joanna?"

Cathy rolls her eyes. "Never to their faces because they terrified me as a child, but they're gossipy women who sit around needling into other people's lives."

My lips tip at the edges. "Who're they trying to set you up with?"

"The new science teacher at the High School. He's smart, I'll give them that, but he's also divorced with a ten-year-old daughter and fifteen years older than me. No, thank you."

"Oh, Cathy," I say in sympathy.

She raises her glass in pity toast. "Yes, they've given up on me." She clears her throat. "Dinner's ready." She pushes a plate of chicken and rice to me.

I take it happily and settle in front of the TV. We watch "The Holiday Calendar" and eat in peaceful harmony until a piano melody begins from the adjacent wall.

"Here to be the vain of my existence." Cathy puts her plate down and moves to the wall that connects her apartment to her neighbor. "Keep it down!" She bangs her fist on the wood, making some of her frames shake.

"You keep it down," he responds in a muffle voice.

"Is this every night?" I ask, sipping on my hot chocolate.

It's finally cold enough to drink comfortably. Adding marshmallows and chocolate drizzles is Cathy's twist on my recipe. She's lucky she doesn't have a sugar problem by now with the amount of sweets she eats.

As we continue to watch the movie, the music from next door continues to flow.

She pulls a pillow to her face and grunts loudly. "He's impossible."

"I'm actually very tired. Going to bed will help me recuperate from the jetlag." I stretch, then give my friend a hug goodnight.

Before I get to bed, I check my emails. I use the light from the screen to read my Christmas list one more time. The best place to find inspiration for a new town tradition will be in the other traditions. This feels like the most natural thing to do. I fold the paper and close my eyes. Tomorrow will be a great day.

Chapter Two

I stare at the old bank bones with far more appreciation than anyone else in this room. When I see places like these, I don't see the potential in dollar signs. I should. That's what makes the world go round, but I see history. Most importantly, how I can be part of the restoration.

I think my love for restoring and preserving history was born from my father's influence. There's nothing in this world he can't fix. His words, not mine. He sure tried everything. All items that ever crossed his path found a second life.

"What do you think, Mark?" the mayor asks me.

He hired me a year ago to give the town a new life within their old bones. I've never been in a town so full of charm and beautifully preserved buildings. My job is to help keep their charm as they get remodeled and move up to code. For some buildings, it's their first time being open to the public in years.

"Mr. Robles, this building might be our biggest job and

the most impressive renovation," I say, and I mean every word.

He looks around the room like he sees what I see. I'm sure the view from where we both stand is much different. His priority is to make Maples attractive to the tourists that keep our economy going.

"I can see this place turning into an event center for all town functions. It'll give us an indoor space with breathtaking architecture." He gestures at the columns. "Look at that moulding."

"Stunning," I agree.

"Hello," a voice calls from the doorway.

Mrs. Robles gives her husband a wave and a look that means business. This is just supposed to be a quick stop to look at what we have as we wrap up another project around the corner.

"Late for dinner," Mr. Robles says with a sheepish smile.

"I'll send you a project proposal for all the changes by next week," I say.

Mr. Robles takes my hand for a firm shake. "That'll be perfect."

I follow him outside and wait for him to lock the doors behind us. Mrs. Robles is behind the wheel with the car already waiting at the curb.

"Would you like to join us for dinner, Mark?" She asks.

I appreciate the offer of a home cooked meal. Half of my weekly meals come from the frozen aisle. Sadly, I've got to shake my head because if I veer from my prearranged plans for the night, I would never hear the end of it.

Every Tuesday in Maples, Maine, inside Ricky's Bar, about half of the town meets for bingo. That's where I've been every Tuesday since I first arrived. I met the iconic duo of Patty and Joanna in my first month here, and I've known nothing else since then. I'm part of their book club, bingo squad, and if I didn't put my foot down, I'd also be part of their knitting club.

I spot Patty and Joanna at their regular table the second I walk inside. I try to socialize outside their circle now and then. I haven't gotten the chance to talk to Romo in a while. He owns the bar, which was previously owned by his father "Ricky". I'm sure if he could, he would've gotten rid of bingo night years ago. The event is beloved by the town to the point that soon enough it'll be hard to walk around.

Romo is hard at work behind the bar when I catch his attention. He has three other employees helping him, but as always, the place is already filling up for Bingo night.

"Your usual?" he asks.

I nod, and he hands me a cold beer with a frosty rim. Despite the cold outside, the inside is toasty, making the liquid go down smoothly.

"Did you regret hosting Thanksgiving dinner?" I ask, taking a sip of my drink.

"It's fine," he says and looks around. "I might host a Christmas one."

At that comment, the mug freezes in my hand midway to my mouth. He catches my reaction and shrugs. Suddenly finding something to wipe on the bar top.

"I didn't know so many people would come. Makes me wonder what they were doing before, you know?"

I can't fight the shit-eating grin on my face. It's just that this grumpy man has nothing nice to say about the people out here. Everything and everyone seems to be a nuisance, but I'm catching on that is just how Romo is.

Romo picks up my beer mug and wipes under it. "You could use a coaster." He rumbles as he turns around.

"Mark." Patty waves me in her direction.

"I've avoided my faith for too long," I joke.

Romo says nothing else as I take my drink to Patty's table. When I'm a few steps away, I realize Joanna isn't the only one sitting with her. A young woman with brown hair and the most stunning smile chuckles at the two older women. My body moves to the table and takes the one open chair available while my mind catches up.

"This is Rosa. An old friend turns new again," Patty says as she pads Rosa's hand.

"I used to live here, but moved away a year ago. Now I'm back for a little while." Rosa gives me an earnest smile. "I don't remember you from before. Are you new in town?"

I clear my throat. "Yes, the mayor hired me to work on a beautification project for the town."

"He's helping restore some of the old buildings to reopen." Patty passes bingo cards to the table. "They've reopened the old post office."

"I saw that." Rosa beams. "You did that?"

"That's what I do," I say and smile with a little pride.

The heat rising to my cheeks is completely unprovoked and I can't help but press the back of my palms against them to cool them down. I take a bigger gulp of my beer, hoping that'll help.

"That sounds fascinating," Rosa says. "What project is next?"

"Well, the courthouse is having some updates done, but the next big one will be the old bank."

I try to stop fussing with my hands by clamping them together under the table. Patty and Joanna take turns describing the inside of the bank. They gush over the old details that had the mayor and me excited about this project.

"I've never seen it, but it sounds stunning." Rosa looks

over at her bingo card. "I must've just missed you when you arrived in town last year."

"Yeah," I say, looking over my card. "I've been here for almost a year."

We're drawn to the mic at the back of the room as someone announces the beginning of bingo. I'd be worried that Patty and Joanna would be listening in on our conversation if I didn't know their attention zeros in on their cards when the numbers get called.

"What brings you back?" I ask Rosa.

"I'm not sure. I travel a lot and something inside me really missed Maples. Of course, also my friend Cathy."

"Oh, how's Cathy?" I ask her.

"Very upset with these two." Rosa gives Patty and Joanna a side eye that goes completely unnoticed.

"Is this about bad matchmaking attempts?" I chuckle.

Rosa's eyes widened. "Is it intentional?"

"When have they ever done something that wasn't intentional?"

I get two numbers on a roll and mark them on my bingo card. Roy Grey is the trusty caller every Tuesday. He's a crowd favorite because of his speed, or lack thereof. I've never been more glad for him than today.

"Sheriff Thompson." Patty waves him over. "Lazy night?"

The joke is because nothing ever happens in Maples, and every night is a lazy night. However, this time, the sheriff doesn't laugh with the rest of us.

"As a matter of fact, this is the second night that someone moves Christmas decorations from one house to another." He looks over the room as if trying to spot the culprit amongst the bingo players.

"That's awful." Joanna gives him a reassuring nod. "You'll find them very soon."

"That I will," he says and scowls at both Rosa and me before departing to survey the room from another angle.

"I think we're suspects," I tell Rosa.

"Everyone who wasn't born here is a suspect, according to Johnny Thompson."

She says his name with little care for the sheriff. Before today I had nothing but pleasant interactions with the young man. He's young for his title, but I figured that's what happens in small towns. I believe his father was once sheriff, and he followed in his footsteps. The youngest one ever elected, if I recall correctly.

"Do you know him?" I ask Rosa.

"He dated Cathy in High School. I inherited her long time hate for him when we became best friends."

"Girls stick together." Joanna nods.

"Exactly." Patty taps the table then lends in close. "Any guesses on who's behind the decorations moving?"

"There are too many options. Johnny has his hands full this time." Joanna shakes her head.

"Whatever kids are moving decorations around should know that won't stick if making a new tradition is what they hope to accomplish." Patty shrugs.

"I'm not the only one trying to start a new Christmas tradition, I see," Rosa says with a frown.

"Every year there are many attempts, sweetheart, but don't you give up." Patty squeezes her hand.

"I think I missed something." I look between the women at the table. "What does the recent vandalism have to do with Christmas traditions?"

"The town has several traditions they carry out every year," Rosa says while she pulls out a piece of paper from her pocket.

I've noticed the Christmas spirit in town is excessive. In a good way. I grew up with a mother who said if her front yard didn't look like Christmas threw up on it, then it wasn't ready. Seeing all the holiday spirit in Maples felt like home.

"Every so often, a very good one gets started, and the town adopts it as a whole. The last tradition was added in 2013." Rosa passes me the piece of paper.

"Oh yeah, the snow shovel," Joanna says. "It was a good one."

"Romo started it," Patty explains. "He used to go on Christmas eve and shovel a couple of folks' driveways so they could go in and out of their places." Patty grins as if it's the cutest thing a grown man can do. "The town adopted the tradition and now volunteers with the fire department provide shovel services to the town."

I turn to look at my friend behind the bar and have only a little difficulty believing he got a tradition started. There are plenty of layers to Romo.

I unfold the paper Rosa handed me and see she has a Christmas list going.

"And you want to create one too?" I ask her.

"These are all the current traditions. I figured the best way to find a new one is to partake in the existing ones."

"I like it." I hand her the paper back. "You got the first step down."

Rosa leans back in her chair, proud to be on the right track. As plans go, it doesn't sound too bad.

"You should help her," Patty says. "It's the gentleman's thing to do."

"Two minds think better than one." Joanna crosses her arms and nods.

I gape between the two women because I feel like I walked right into that one. I really should know better. They never say anything without reason. Didn't I tell Rosa just that a couple of minutes ago?

"Rosa never asked me to join her on this adventure," I say sheepishly. "It's an intrusion for you two to imply otherwise."

I give Rosa a smile to convey we're off the hook, but her eyes are saying the opposite.

"I wouldn't mind the help," she says with an eager smile.

I might be reading into this and she just wants to be polite. I'm a complete stranger she met not even an hour ago. There's no way she wants me to help her with this Christmas tradition thing.

"It's okay," I say and look back to see how many bingo numbers I've missed.

"Oh, okay. Well, if you change your mind, I'd love the help," she says and looks back down at her bingo card. "The lord knows I need all the help I can get."

"Are you sure?" I whisper the question to her with furrowed brows.

"You might be the only person in this town other than Romo who doesn't care about coming up with their own Christmas tradition."

We both look over our shoulders at my friend behind the bar.

"He scares me," Rosa finishes.

She's accurate in her assessment that I have zero interest in partaking. I make eye contact with Patty and Joanna and both whisper-yell at me gibberish.

"I'm free tomorrow if you'd like to start soon," I say to Rosa.

I hold my breath as Rosa's eyes rise from her paper to meet mine. I gasp for air, stunned by Rosa's gaze. Her smile is bright and worth every discomfort this little mission will ensue.

Chapter Three

The hustle and bustle of the streets gives me a kind of energy I can't explain. It doesn't work in other towns I've stayed in like it does here. Maybe that's the reason I'm back to Maples. Despite my perpetual drifting, the current of this town has an electric field that pulls me in.

I scan the crowds for Mark again but come out empty. Christmas music drifts to my ears. It adds a beat to my step. I got here early, so it's not like he's late. I can't deny that I'm eager to see Mark again. He's handsome and speaks with an air of someone wise beyond his years. That's why I jumped at the idea of him helping.

"Hey, stop that!"

I look up to see a cop scolding a group of teenagers. They stand there sheepishly and listen as she explains how each person needs to take turns dumping trash to not make a mess. I chuckle to myself when I realize the scatter of cups on the ground is from them. This town is nothing if not a neat upkeep.

I move to the opposite side of the downtown square, looking at the market stands. I know I told Mark I'd wait for him, but I can't help myself. The actual activity is getting a Christmas ornament to add to your tree. I don't even have a tree, so I'd be using Cathy's for this year's spirit.

It's not long before I spot Mark across the street walking in the opposite direction. He's on the phone talking to someone, which it's probably why he isn't answering my texts.

I put down the ornament I'm looking at and decide to save Mark from looking for me. I put a little speed into my step to reach him and slow down when we're side by side. He's so focused on his call, he doesn't notice me. I try not to make it obvious and eavesdrop. I have to walk twice as fast as I normally would to keep up with his long strives. His genetics have an unfair advantage on my five foot three inch frame.

I'm paying so much attention to leg pace matching his that I don't see the mother with the stroller coming directly at me. She isn't looking at me either as her toddler is outside the stroller, pulling her arm towards the window shop showcasing nutcracker toys.

I try to stop, I really do, but it's too late. The next thing I know I'm tumbling down and I'm taking that stroller with me. There's an echo of "Oh nos!" as I hit the ground. I stretch my arms in front of me, holding onto the stroller's fabric in an attempt to keep my weight off it. The last thing I need is to break someone's stroller in the middle of the street.

"Are you okay?" the mother asks, clutching her toddler to her chest.

This is a small town, but thankfully I don't recognize

the young mom. If I'm lucky, she's a tourist visiting town for the lights.

"Of course," I say, way more chirpy than I feel.

I try to get up, and a ping of pain radiates from my bottom. That's definitely going to bruise. I wonder if Cathy has arnica for it. To add to my complete humiliation, Mark didn't keep walking. The handsome stranger is stretching his hand towards me and my first reaction is to shutter away. The earth is welcome to swallow me whole.

"How's the view of the market from down there?" Mark asks me, pocketing his phone.

I climb to my feet on my own and fight the urge to cry. The agony of the fall fares nothing to the hit on my ego.

"Let's make the rest of today quick and painless," I say.

My voice sounds steady. Better than the way I feel inside.

"I see," Mark says. He gestures for me to lead the way. "What's the first thing on your list?"

"Well, I knocked things off the list yesterday before Bingo. The one I want to accomplish today is the Christmas market ornament." I gesture to the opposite side of the square. "Ross has a store on the other side where people can make their own ornaments."

"That sounds like fun." Mark walks in that direction.

"It's a nice twist to the tradition of getting a new ornament every year. If you make it, it's a little more special," I say.

We make it to the store just in time to take the last outdoor table for our crafts. Ross is delighted to have more people choose his version of Christmas ornament. I stop myself from telling him he didn't invent painting wood pieces in the shape of ornaments. But I'm glad when I hear Patty tell him after she arrives to join us.

Ross has just about everything in his store. There's no way to describe this place as anything other than its name. "Everything's Here." Lazy really, but no one would accuse Ross of being a hard worker.

"You're handy with paint," I tell Mark.

He has painted a wooden soldier with red and green colors decorated with golden feathers.

"Painting anything for a Christmas tradition is out of the question?" he asks.

I nod my head. "I don't possess that talent." To prove my statement, I turn my ornament his way.

He gives me a sympathetic smile. I can tell he wants to lie to me and say it's not that bad.

"I know it's ugly cute and I can live with that." I turn it back to me and continue painting.

"Let me look at your list one more time. Every time I think of something, I look and it's already there."

I pass it to him. "The list is full and plentiful," I say.

I plan on knocking as many as I can in a day to make the most of it. I also think this is the way I can get the most inspiration.

"I see you crossed off visiting Santa." he taps the paper. "I was looking forward to that one since I've never been."

"Yeah, it was the first thing I got off my list," I say, then pause. "Wait, you've never visited Santa?"

Mark chuckles to himself. "I can't believe they let you sit on his lap."

"You need to visit Santa," I say with determination.

This is no longer just about me. If Mark is going to help with this, it's only fair he gets through some of the list as well.

"Mr. Jorge dresses as Santa in town. I won't ask that old man to let me sit on his lap." Mark whisper-shouts, "that's ridiculous."

He might be right about that. I also doubt Mr. Jorge will let him. He has a shorter limit for bullshit than the rest of us. I do some quick thinking and a very special person comes to mind. I've been meaning to pay him a visit since I'm back.

"We won't go to Santa in town. I have to go to the next town over, anyway. You'll be great company. We can visit Santa there."

"No way," Mark shakes his head. "What makes you think that Santa will do it?"

"Hey." I straighten my back. "This is not the attitude. Are you with me to complete this Christmas list?"

"Well, yes," he says, but shakes his head. "But."

"None of that. We'll worry about hurdles when we get there."

"Rosa," he tries to reason as a cute blush colors his cheeks.

"Imagine the things we can find as we cross every item on this list. We don't know what will spark the idea that forever brands us as pioneers of this town."

"Your level of gaslighting is impressive."

My face breaks into a victorious smile. "Let's go make history."

His smile is as big and wide as mine as he says, "Let's go."

I feel myself blush. "Perfect, then let's put this away and talk about a game plan for tomorrow." I clap my hands.

I get on my feet and gather everything I didn't use on my ornament. I can see the hesitation on his steps as he follows me inside so we can pay and put all our crafts away. Mark is a man of a few words, but he's a great listener. A few times today when I went on talking about everything and anything I assumed he tuned out, but he'd ask me a follow up question from where I left off.

We're waiting in line by the register when the door opens and with a cold gust of air walks in the Sheriff. His eyes scan the room before they land on Mark and me. Johnny makes a beeline for us.

"Where have you two been?" Johnny asked in a serious tone.

No greeting or welcoming.

"Around here." Mark looks at me with an arch brow.

I share his amusement at the sudden interest from the sheriff.

"They were painting ornaments. Would you like to try your luck at one, Johnny?" Ross asks him with a smile from the register.

"No."

"Are you sure? You haven't done one since you were a child." Ross pushes.

We chuckle.

The sheriff doesn't find it funny and completely ignores Ross. Mark and I get one last glare from him before he leaves.

"Do you have some kind of history with him?" Mark asks me.

No way, I shake my head. "Not besides Cathy's. Do you have some kind of history?"

Mark cuts me off. "Nope."

"Then we're at a loss."

"Don't mind him," Patty says. "You two have a good-night!" She waves at everyone on her way out.

Mark and I pay for our ornaments and head outside. There are so many ideas flying through my mind. The possibilities of it all.

"So, Santa Claus tomorrow?" I ask Mark.

His expression is painful, but I think he has too much pride to back down. His nod is reluctant and stiff, but I don't let that persuade me.

"Do you have a car?" I ask. At his nod, I clap. "Perfect. Pick me up outside the green building tomorrow after you get off work. I'll be waiting!"

Before he can fight me on it, I wrap my arms around his middle and pull him in for a hug. I expect him to stand there stiff as a board, but he quickly melts into me. Mark is a warm ball of fabric that smells of woods and smoke. I'd be happy to stay wrapped around him all day, but I've embarrassed myself enough for one day. I let him step back.

"Tomorrow Mark. Goodnight," I say and start my route home.

"Goodnight," he says and watches me walk the block down home.

"What happened to you?" Cathy asks as I close the door behind me and turn her five security locks on the door. "You look like a mess but happy and all upbeat."

"I look like a mess?"

I look down at my clothes and in the light of the living room I can see streaks of something on my sweater and legging. I don't even want to know what it is since I essentially wiped the sidewalk with my back and bottom.

"You're all smiles, so maybe it was the beating you needed?" Cathy eyes my clothing with concern.

She should be worried. The number of germs I'm dragging inside is a health hazard.

"Despite the floor wiping, I definitely had the best of

days. I met Mark at the Christmas market and got my ornament. We have plans for tomorrow."

I hold the prized possession high in the air. I don't even flinch at Cathy's expression of its ugliness. Walking to the Christmas tree in the corner of the room, I place it on one of the branches.

"With that, I'm off to bed. Tomorrow will be a long day," I say and march my happy self to the bathroom where I can dispose of my clothes properly and clean up.

"Wait a minute!" Cathy shouts after me. "How was Mark? Do you like him? And most importantly, do you know why the old ladies never told me about him?"

I chuckle my way to the bathrooms and shut the door behind me. I can hear her feet follow me, but she knows better than trying to talk to me when the water is running. These old apartments are loud. She smacks the door, then retreats.

Mark knows of Cathy, which means the Bingo club has talked about her. He even knew of her terrible set-up, which means there's something bigger happening for my friend. I plan on figuring that out after I accomplish my plan.

I open my phone and see a message from a new number I haven't saved yet. My heart is fluttering like I'm some teenager. I don't beat myself up about it. It has been that long, and the emotion is almost new to me.

> "Let me know when you make it home. I can't believe I didn't think of walking you home."

> "Made it home. The streets are rough, but not that rough."

> "Might need to burn my clothes after today. Thanks again for helping."

A Jolly Ever After

"Burning them might be a good idea. I'm glad to hear you're home."

"Goodnight Mark."

"Goodnight, Rosa."

Chapter Four

I hang on to Mark's hand for dear life as we make our way down to my favorite Santa spot. Scurrying around people with someone as big and bulky as Mark is hard. I'm able to push myself through small spaces between people, but doing that with Mark is impossible. I've not been cursed at in a while. Northway is about an hour out of Maples and big enough that all small town charm is lost here.

I spot the line outside the store a block out. I sigh and accept my fate. It's not like any other Santa Claus will do, anyway.

I decided not to go into details in hopes Mark wouldn't change his mind. He was right about Santa visiting stations having limits on ages, but I know this particular santa would do anything for an extra twenty. It's also on the way to my tamales spot. I've been dying to come to this side just for them. Two birds and one stone and all that. Also, having some company on the ride here isn't bad at all.

"I haven't been to Northway in a while," Mark says as he looks around.

"Let's get in line before it gets bigger." I gesture forward, and Mark is happy to go along with it.

As time passes, our topics of conversation begin to get odd. However, the fun in each question never ceases.

"If you could be any animal in the world, what would you be and why?" I ask.

"Do the water aliens count?" He eyes me curiously. "They were technically just sea creatures a year or so ago."

"Fair enough." I wave at him to keep going.

"I would definitely want to be one of those so I can see what's out there. What if the reason we never went that far down wasn't because of the pressure or whatever?" He lowers his tone to a whisper. "What if it's because those who made it never came back?"

"You're far too rational for my game!" I groan.

I'm going to have nightmares about these sea creatures now turning aliens for days on end.

"Don't tell me I scared you." He looks me in the eye. "Nothing a smutty alien book can't make you forget."

That'd make the entire idea harmless again, but I don't tell him that. Instead, I huff in indignation.

"I don't read that!" I lie through my teeth and he can see it clear as day. "What do you know about alien romance?"

Mark has been so focused on our conversation that not once has he turned to look at the Santa clause sitting on the chair inside the store. I figured that by now I'd be making explanations, but despite the line moving, he never looked. Until now.

"Rosa," Mark says, looking between me and Pedro.

"Don't be hesitant, he's just a little darker than the one you see on TV." I push him forward and give Pedro a wave. "He's here to fulfill a childhood checkmark, then we'll be on our way."

Pedro shakes his head, but I pull the warm twenty from my back pocket. I hardly ever carry cash, but I stopped at an ATM outside Cathy's place just for this.

"Give him five minutes." I hand Pedro the bill.

He pockets it. "He gets two and he better not wiggle."

Mark looks like a deer in headlights. He's beyond his comfort zone.

"Don't imagine yourself as a thirty-something man sitting on a minimum wage employee. You're a little seven-year-old right now. He's the one who'll be sitting on Santa's lap. Close your eyes if you have to."

"Any weird noise and it's over." Pedro huffs.

"Hush," I say to Santa. "Get in character or I want my money back."

"Ho, ho, ho, who do we have here?"

Pedro is actually good at this. Despite him being forty pounds too skinny to be Santa, he has the rest of the act down.

Mark hesitates but sits on Pedros lap. There's tension on his knees and I swear he's hovering rather than fully sitting on the man. I don't point out that it's part of the experience. I think I've pushed far enough.

"What would you like for Christmas, little boy?" Santa asks, making me giggle.

This is feeling like a bad porno. I swallow the laugh building on my chest. Mark is in this situation because of me. I can't turn on him now by mocking him for it. I snap a photo for memory's sake, but the two of them look tense with forced smiles.

"Back then I thought what I truly wanted was a hot wheels track," Mark tells Santa.

It's easy to imagine little Mark with his big glasses and dimpled smile.

"Did you ever get it?" I ask.

"I did," he says with a sheepish smile. "It was my favorite thing in the world for about a year."

The smile he shoots my way is so genuine and free. I can feel a mirroring one plaster on my face.

"That was three minutes." Pedro ushers us out.

I don't argue with Pedro, because Mark jumped and crossed the room in a blink. I have to speed walk out of the store to meet him on the sidewalk.

"If I'm honest, I don't think this healed any childhood trauma. I think it gave me and Pedro some fresh adult trauma."

I look at the photo I took on my phone, then at Mark. I turn the screen to him and cringe. The laughter I was holding back in there finally erupts from my chest with loud howls.

"It looks like something Facebook would take down if uploaded. There's nothing wrong happening, but it feels dirty, doesn't it?" I ask between laughs.

"That's the definition of blackmail material." He laughs with me in an easy and careless way I uniquely attribute to him.

I wait for him to demand I erase the photo, but he doesn't.

"Where to next?" he asks, looking around.

"Let's grab a drink!"

I link my arm to his and lead the way. There's a bar around the corner and I need to wait for someone to show up before we can start the ride home.

I know we've been at the bar for about an hour when a familiar face steps behind the bar. I look down at my drink and realize I've been so busy talking to Mark that the ice in it is nearly all melted. That's not like me. But it goes to show how much I'm enjoying myself.

"Hey there Pedro," I say in greeting, then pull out my wallet. "I want half a dozen of pork and another half of chicken."

"Wait a minute," Mark points at the once Santa now bartender. "I sat on your lap."

"I'll give you the twenty back if you never say that again," Pedro whispers to Mark over the bar top.

"How rude of me." I tap my forehead. "Would you like some tamales, Mark?" I point at Pedro, who's already looking proud of what I'm about to say. "His grams make the best tamales. I come all the way here to get them. The secret is coconut oil. You can taste it just a bit in the masa, but it's much healthier."

At least that is what I tell myself. I should've looked up the nutritional facts by now, but it will ruin the mystery. Great way to make the consumption of multiple tamales during the holidays guiltless.

"Now my wife makes them. But they are just as good," he hurries to assure me.

That better be true. His grandma was kind enough to give me the recipe when I asked. But that's a lot of work for only six tamales that I eat in a week. I might reconsider if I had a family to feed, but for myself, making a trip here is the best choice.

"Why not?" Mark looks at me with something in his eyes. "If you sing their praises, I'll have to try them." He turns to Pedro. "I'll have the same as she's having."

As we wait for our order to be ready, we fall back into easy conversation. I find myself seeking to hear Mark's laugh. The inner comedian inside me makes a special appearance. Just to get my fix. It's addicting. I tell myself to tone it down.

"This is your total love birds," Pedro taps the bill on the counter.

Mark puts down his card before I can think and then Pedro hands us two bags.

"Off we go," Mark says.

The trip back flies by. One minute I'm talking about my special hot chocolate recipe and the next we are parking outside my building.

"You don't need to walk me upstairs," I say before Mark can unbuckle.

"Are you sure?" he asks.

"Of course. After all, knowing how Johnny has it out for us, he's probably hiding in the bushes, ready to pounce once you leave the car in the loading zone and have it towed."

Mark looks around the street to make sure Johnny wasn't hiding about.

"It's a joke Mark," I say.

I pad his hand before opening the door and climbing out. He chuckles, but the smile doesn't reach his eyes. He remains alert, his eyes sharp in our surroundings.

"What's the plan for tomorrow?" He asks as I stand outside the door.

I stand there and shuffle from foot to foot. I hadn't thought about this far enough. At least not past today. After the emotions of today, I'm a bit brain dead to think of something on the spot.

"I'll let you know when I figure it out. You've got to work in the morning anyway, right?"

He nods.

"Then that's settled."

I begin to push the door close when he raises his hand to stop me.

"Wait," he says, then pauses as if thinking better of it.

"Mark?" I tilt my head to see him better inside the car. "I'm freezing my limbs off here."

"Send me a photo of the remaining items on your list. I'll plan something for us to knock off."

The smile that finds its way to my face is earnest. A man who can make plans without being prompted. I might've found the last one left alive.

"Really?" I ask.

It's on the tip of my tongue to say he doesn't have to do that. This is my adventure he's embarking on. But it feels good to know I don't have to think of everything.

"Yes," he says with determination.

"Thank you," I say. Heat warms my chest.

"Goodnight Rosa."

"Goodnight Mark."

Chapter Five

I make quick work of completing everything that needs to be done early in the morning. I've all emails and phone calls made before noon. Thankfully, in my profession, most of the foremen I work with are up by five in the morning. By the time I wake up and start my day, they're having their second breakfast. Only a few of them sounded surprised to hear from me so early.

Once I'm done at the office, I make a quick stop at the supermarket in town to prepare for tonight's plans.

Rosa sent me the remaining items on her list late last night. The lack of items left on the list made today's plan limited. However, there's one item in particular I think I can make special on that list.

I pause my shopping when I spot a blue coat in the produce section of the market.

"Patty," I say.

The woman is smelling a bag of apples when her eyes find me.

"Hey sweetheart," she says with a smile.

I cross my arms and give her a look.

"Don't tell me you're mad we bent your arm into helping Rosa with that list. The girl is a cutie."

"Your setting-up ways will never change, will they?" I ask her.

She hoots in laughter.

"Don't tell me you have complaints. You two are the talk of the town. Everyone thinks you're cute going around town completing the Christmas list." She claps her hands.

"Everyone knows about the list, huh?"

This won't make coming up with a new tradition any easier. With eyes on us, it might all get harder. We're not the only ones wanting to come up with an addition to the list. I remember last year how many people tried their luck.

"Some hope for a new tradition to add. Something new to do. Others hope this will entice Rosa to stay for good."

"Rosa's like the wind, unstoppable and endless."

I never understood before when people describe others as bigger than life, but that's what Rosa is. There's no way to keep her somewhere because she's everything all at once.

Patty gives me a gentle look. "Everyone needs a home. That doesn't mean that home needs to be a cage," she says.

"I'll do my best to help her complete the list, but I can't guarantee she'll want to stay."

"Let me know if there's anything I can do to help," Patty says.

I'm under no illusion that Rosa will stay past Christmas, but she keeps coming back for a reason. Maybe if she builds enough ties to this town, she won't ever want to leave again. A small part of me wants to try.

"As a matter of fact." I gesture to the items in my basket. "Have you made these yet?"

Patty's smile is bright. "Bring Rosa by tonight. Bring Cathy too and Romo. Everyone should be there by seven."

She takes the ingredients off my cart and passes them to hers.

"Are you sure?"

"Don't be foolish. I wouldn't make the invitation otherwise. Also, remember the lake behind my house?"

I nod.

"It's frozen solid during this time." She winks.

The clicking of boots has us both turning to the fast approaching sheriff.

"I didn't see you in town last night," he says to me with a glare already on his face. "As a matter of fact, you and Rosa weren't accounted for."

"We were in Northway," I say.

"I'm guessing you have witnesses that will vouch for you?"

"Am I under arrest?" I arch a brow.

This little accusatory routine is getting old and offensive. Rosa and I aren't criminals and being insinuated that we are is getting on my nerves.

"Not. Yet," he seethes.

"Oh Johnny, chew on a Tums before you give yourself heartburn. Leave Mark and Rosa alone. Everyone will be at my place tonight at seven. Stop by and pick up some food." Patty pads his chest soothingly. "You need some homemade food to release all this tense indigestion."

He doesn't answer Patty as he walks away from us.

"Don't mind him," Patty tells me. "See you tonight." She waves and pushes her card to another section of the market.

I pull into the parking lot of the green building five past five. Cathy is walking out of the building as I approach the entrance.

"Hey Cathy," I say.

She stops when she spots me and tilts her head.

I extend my hand out when I recall we haven't officially met. "I'm Mark."

She takes my hand and shakes it. "I thought tonight started at seven." She looks at her wristwatch. "You're here two hours early."

I texted Rosa to spread the word of tonight's invite. I contacted Romo, who told me in no simple terms he wasn't going.

"I have a small stop before Patty's." I chuckle and scratch the back of my head.

Cathy looks up at the sky, then back at me. "I was hoping I could ride with you and avoid driving in this weather."

"You can't leave with us right now?" I ask, hoping she says no.

I want to take advantage of Patty's frozen lake. I saw Rosa had ice skating on her list. She hasn't gone to the one in town because it hasn't been opened yet. The mayor mentioned in passing how it will open in a week. I've never been skating and trying my luck for the first time in front of the whole town sounds like a major mistake. Like this, only Patty's neighbors will laugh at me.

"Romo will go too," I say, trying my luck. "You can probably leave with him."

The bar is not that far a walk from here. About a block down the street. From what I gathered during my time here is that Romo has a soft spot for Cathy. Everytime she comes around, he's quick to help with anything she needs. I doubt he won't agree to at least drive her to dinner.

"Perfect." Cathy nods. "I'll see you there."

I knock on Cathy's door twice before Rosa rushes to pull the door open.

"Sorry I'm so early," I say, but I see she's ready.

"I saw you talking to Cathy outside, so I figured you had something in mind for us to do."

I pull my backpack in front of me and unzip it to show her what I've in mind. A squeal of excitement is Rosa's only response.

"I think I might love when you do that," I say.

She beams at the compliment. "Cathy hates it, so it's nice to hear someone else likes it."

Patty lives a little outside of town, but not too far. I can see why Cathy didn't want to drive out here if she can avoid it. The streets are narrow and covered in snow. There's no way Romo isn't bringing her over, even if she wasn't Cathy.

"Where did you get the skates?" Rosa asks while pulling the two pairs out of my bag.

I glance at her in my passenger seat. "Ross really has everything in his store."

"That man is ready for a zombie apocalypse." Rosa pauses at the sight of Patty's home. "Patty lives here, and she used to make me share my bingo winnings with her."

"She still makes me split mine with her."

Rosa gives me a side look. "You've been here before?"

"I volunteer to shovel people's driveways."

Her smile is teasing. "You partake in Romos Christmas tradition."

I gesture to the Christmas list on her lap. "We'll knock that one out together later this month."

The idea that we'll still be doing these weeks later is exhilarating. Imagining a future with Rosa is easy.

"Deal!" She claps her hands.

I take the larger pair of skates in hand. "Do you know how to do this?"

"We shouldn't put them on here." She opens her door and gestures out to the side of Patty's house. "Let's go."

It's not long before Patty comes outside with a steaming mug of coffee to sit on a chair and watch me make a complete fool out of myself. I notice how she puts the cup away when she laughs too hard at me. I don't even want to check and see if any of her neighbors are also having a good time at my expense.

"When you said you were bad, I thought you were being modest," Rosa says between laughter.

She has been laughing so hard that air is all that comes out at times. I swear I saw a little tear coming down her cheek, but she was quick to wipe it away.

"I was being honest," I say and climb back to my feet.

Rosa takes a step back from me. She tried to help me stay up at first, but quickly learned that didn't help. We both ended up on the floor within minutes.

"You skate and show me how it's done." I gesture for her to leave.

"Just for a little bit." She gestures with her fingers that she'll be gone for a moment.

She turns towards the middle of the lake and sways away. Her movements are graceful and soft. She turns and skates from one edge of the opening to the other one, catching speed as she goes.

I shuffle my way back to the edge and find Cathy and Romo standing next to Patty on the patio.

"She's a natural," Patty says.

"That she is." I turn back and see Rosa is still skating, unperturbed by the audience.

"This was your before dinner adventure?" Cathy asks me with a mysterious tone.

Her expression doesn't tell me how she feels about it either way.

"Yes," I say tentatively.

I look over her shoulder at Romo, who's scowling at me, but I think that has more to do with the way I tricked him into coming here.

"That was very nice of you. I'm sure she truly appreciates it." She steps close into my space and I have to look down to meet her eyes. "Don't mess with my friend because I'll answer for her."

"He won't," Romo says and pulls her back to the front of his chest.

I give him a nod of appreciation, but he rolls his eyes at me.

Cathy looks over her shoulder at him. "I'll be the judge of that."

The doorbell rings, and Patty gets up from her chair. "That must be Joanna. Let's go get started. We'll be baking cookies while we eat dinner, then we'll decorate them once they are out of the oven."

Patty rushes inside, and Cathy follows her with a smile. Romo stays standing there with a glare directed at me. I'm about to apologize when Cathy calls for him from inside. The big softy sighs and goes inside.

I turn and wait for Rosa on the threshold.

Chapter Six

I've been doing everything wrong. That's the only conclusion I have as we walk out of Patty's house with leftovers in plastic containers. Our stomachs are full and happy.

"We have one last stop." Mark takes my hand in his and squeezes it tightly.

"We got to make and decorate cookies with Patty, not to mention the ice skating. You got two things off the list already. Can there possibly be more?"

"Just one more," he says with a devious grin.

I lean back on the car seat and take it all in. This is far more amazing than I could've planned. I can tell from the glances shot my way that Cathy's going to have many questions for me. Thankfully, she'll be going to Ricky's Bar after Patty's. Romo promised her a spiced eggnog she couldn't stop talking about over dinner.

If I'm lucky, I'll be asleep by the time she makes it home. I don't think I'm ready to talk about what's going on or what this list has turned into. If I talk about it with Cathy, I'll have to face it too, and I'm just not ready yet.

We stop in front of a boarded up building a couple of blocks away from the town square.

"What's this?" I try to look out of the window, but the trees around cover most of the building from sight.

"Remember how I mentioned the bank being the next project?" Mark asks.

"Are we going to see it?" I whisper.

"Very quickly." Mark rounds the car to open my door. "My lady." He extends his hand to me, and I take it.

We link hands as we walk to a side door. Mark pulls a key from his pocket and opens the door. We make our way inside into the grand foyer of the building.

"This place could be spectacular for weddings," I say in awe.

Massive walls with windows at the top surround the main entrance. Granite floors and wall to ceiling columns frame the space.

"I think the Mayor has something like that in mind, amongst other things."

Mark walks to one side of the room and prompts his phone on a table. He clicks something on and music blurts out of his phone speaker. Darlene Love's voice echoes in the space beautifully and festively.

"Let's get one more thing off your list tonight," Mark says and takes my hand.

My brain is trying to catch up with what's happening when he pulls me to his chest and begins to sway us from side to side. All the tension in my body falls as I lean against him. I press my cheek against the warmth of his chest. I can almost hear his heart beating against my face.

"This is nice," he says with his nose in my hair.

"It is," I say, looking up at him. "I could stay here all night."

"You can stay as long as you want, Rosa."

The words "I want to stay" are about to leave my lips when a rustle of footsteps echo from the front door.

"Maples Police," someone calls.

"Is that who I think it is?" I whisper to Mark.

"Let's go," he whispers back and shuts his phone quickly. "To the back door we came from. Hurry."

Mark takes my hand in his and hurries us out of the building before Johnny can catch up to us. I hold back a giggle in my throat. What are the odds?

I try to make little to no noise as I close the apartment door behind me and lean against it. Once inside, I see the living room is illuminated by the light of the TV.

"That look is trouble." Cathy points at my face from her place on the couch.

The TV is blasting some rerun of Gilmore Girls on full volume. Knowing my friend as well as I do this means she isn't having the best of days. She's infamous for rewatching comfort shows to escape whatever inconvenience God throws her way. No strong soldiers here.

"Beyond in trouble," I say and join her on the couch.

She hands me a cup of yellow liquid. I sniff the rim and realize it's eggnog. I take a small sip and look at the cup.

"Why does it taste like this?"

There's something different in this recipe.

"Romo makes this one especially for me. He adds spices."

"That's very good." I nod.

"There's more in the fridge. Now let's focus on the topic at hand." She taps my knee with a gentle smile that doesn't belong on her face. "Tell mama what's wrong." Her mocking tone is clear as day.

"You're mean!" I push her off me.

"Sorry!" She grabs the remote and mutes the show. She turns her torso to face me. "Please tell me what's wrong and how I can help."

"You can't help and technically, there isn't anything wrong. Everything's the opposite." I cover my face with my hands.

"Opposite," she says and pulls my hands back.

"I really like him," I say.

I can describe my feelings for him beyond that. He's the most amazing person I've had the pleasure of meeting. Meeting him was like meeting a version of me I didn't know existed in another person. He feels like the childhood best friend who makes every day the best day. My cheeks heat just thinking about it. There's no way I can say that much out loud.

Cathy stares at me, waiting for me to go on.

"I really like him. I really like how I fit with him. It's effortless, but not meaningless. The opposite, like it's everything all at once. "

"I see," she says and leans back on the couch. "Do you think you can give me a loan from that lottery ticket you won and find so troubling?"

"Cathy!" I growl. "This wouldn't be a problem for someone else. Someone normal, but it's a problem for me because I'm not normal."

"The horns really give you away, but luckily everyone wears hats in the winter. You have a couple of more months till he's forced to see them."

"Be serious, please!" I throw my head back on the couch.

"You be serious Rosa. What're you afraid of?"

"That I won't want to stay forever. That something will come along and the urge will kick in and I can't do that. I like him so much that I'll hate me if I hurt him."

"Do you think you'll want to leave?" Cathy asks in a soft tone.

"I fear the day will come." Tears gather in my eyes. "I'm a drifter. I've no roots that ground me anywhere. That's all I've ever known."

"It's never too late to change. We are ever evolving. Our best days aren't here yet. That always gives me hope." Cathy leans her head on my shoulder.

At that very moment, piano notes flow through the room.

"Are you going to yell at him?" I ask, looking at the neighbor's wall. "It's quite beautiful, you know."

"Of course I know," she says.

Cathy gets up and walks to the living room window. She flicks the lights off, then cracks the window open just enough to let more of the melody in. She lays back down next to me with only the light coming from the streets to illuminate the space.

"The infuriating asshole is incredibly talented," she says to the dark space.

We sit there in silence, taking in the melody note by note. Allowing the night to fade away with any of the worries that may rise again with the sun.

Chapter Seven

I'm watching a Cinderella Story on Disney when the front door opens and Cathy finally gets home. She works from home most days, but she loves to stretch out her errands to different days and go out at least once a day. Sounds healthy to me.

I get up and check on the milk heating on the stovetop.

"What's happening here?" Cathy joins me in the kitchen.

"Did you bring what I asked?"

She pulls two to-go cups from the convenient store.

"I plan on sharing the deliciousness of Abuelita chocolate." I gesture at the stove.

"Rosa style makes all the difference." Cathy takes a peek at the mixture brawling and gives it an approving nod. "And you're watching a classic."

She drops the bags she was carrying on the kitchen island and rushes to her room. She returns in her pajamas and plonks on the couch.

I look at my watch. "I'm about to head out, but if you wish to keep watching, you can."

I pour the hot drink into the two travel cups and top them with some whipped cream. It'll be a challenge to carry them all the way to Bingo, but I want Mark to try it. I even added hot chocolate to my Christmas list to make the moment even more memorable.

I double check I have everything I need before getting back to the kitchen to get the cups. I watch as the guitar falls off the wall in the movie, revealing the inspirational words behind the wallpaper. My favorite part.

"I love this movie." Cathy looks away from the movie long enough to inspect my clothes. "You look nice. All this for bingo?"

"Yes."

I try to hide the heat rising up my face at the truth. Sue me for trying to look nice for Mark.

"That's nice. Have fun." She gives me a wave.

There's a knock at the front door. Cathy pauses the movie and shoots me a look from the couch. I'm not expecting visitors, so I shrug. She gets up and moves to open the door.

"Hey Mark," Cathy says and opens the door wider.

He steps inside and looks between us. I didn't expect him to pick me up since Ricky's Bar is only a block walk away.

"I figured we can walk together," Mark says, reading my mind. He turns to Cathy. "You aren't coming to bingo?"

Taking in her appearance should be answer enough.

"I have a date with my couch and a movie," she says and makes a beeline to the couch.

"Oh no, please join us. Bingo is one of the few town events you can't miss." He shoots me a look for help.

"It's always fun, but you don't need me to tell you that.

I go every week for a reason." I raise both hands up because that says enough.

"There's a rumor that Romo made even more of that spiked eggnog," Mark says as a persuasion tactic.

"Spiced eggnog. He doesn't add alcohol. He adds spices," Cathy explains.

Mark makes a face.

"It's not bad," I say.

"I'll have to try it." He looks back at Cathy. "Only if you come too."

"Fine," she lifts her hands in surrender.

"What?" I gape at my friend.

"Color me curious," she says, then winks my way.

She definitely agreed to go to give me a hard time. I put on a brave face. Cathy's not cruel, but I definitely feel more on edge knowing she'll be next to me and Mark all night. She can see right through me and whatever crush I'm nursing at the moment. She already knows how I feel about him. I don't need her trying to persuade me one way or another.

We wait for Cathy to change and head over to bingo. It's not until we're about to walk inside the bar that I remember the hot chocolate I left in the kitchen.

"I made us hot chocolate, but forgot it at home," I say to Mark.

"It'll still be good after Bingo tonight," Cathy says over her shoulder as we walk inside.

"That's true, I guess." I pull off my jacket and hang it on my arm.

"Are you sure?" Mark asks. "We can get it now if you wish."

I shake my head. "She's right. We can get it later tonight."

This also gives me an excuse to extend my outing with Mark.

Bingo night is always intense, but when one person wins more than once, it becomes grave. It's as if the entire room has a common enemy and unless that person is cunning enough to take everyone on, things can get out of hand quickly.

My best friend is all smiles as she wins her third game on a roll. There were two other winners before her, but even they're shooting arrows her way at the moment. Everyone cheered after her first win. People booed after her second win. She just called her third win, and the room remained dangerously quiet.

"I forgot why I ever stopped coming to Bingo nights." Cathy's smile is short-lived when the first salt shaker is tossed across the room, nearly missing her head.

There's an echo of loud hollering followed by shoving. My eyes go frantic looking around. I might need to dive in and cover Cathy with my body.

"That's it!" Romo climbs atop the bar and cups his hands around his mouth. "Everyone out. You will not return till you learn how to behave."

"A dinner and a show." Patty stands up, fanning her face. "I love bingo nights."

"Will he really cancel Bingo night?" I ask.

This town lives for Tuesday nights. I can't imagine what it'll be like if we didn't have this to connect over.

An echo of "nos" follows my question.

"Romo's just upset that Cathy's hair was misplaced." Patty hooks her arm to Joannas.

Joanna laughs. "Remember how last week someone pulled the chair from under Ross after winning twice? He said nothing as Ross shouted obscenities from the floor."

"Ross stayed on the floor for a whole other game before someone decided to help him up," Patty adds.

The ladies hoot into laughter again as the memory comes back to mind. I move to follow them out of the bar when I notice Cathy hasn't moved from the table. She stands there frozen in place, staring after the old ladies.

"Cathy," I say.

She snaps from her thoughts and looks over at Romo. He's behind the register, closing taps. Her eyes look at him in a new way. As if she's finally seeing him for the first time.

"Go without me. I'll see you home," she says.

Mark takes my hand in his and leads me out of the bar.

"Did that just happen?" Mark chuckles.

"I'm partly confused," I say.

"Everything looks so beautiful and quiet this late at night, doesn't it?" He says, looking around.

The streets are empty, all but for those exiting the bar. Christmas lights decorate every available surface, including all the storefronts.

We walk slowly hand in hand across the street, looking at the lights. The night feels full of energy despite the calm atmosphere around.

Mark pauses in the middle of the road, looking at the front of a store.

"I got it," Mark says.

"You got what?" I stop and turn to face him.

The gift shop across the street has captured his attention. I try to see what's new that caught his eye, but nothing looks different. There's a Christmas tree with a unique light pattern on display. It can't be the light display. Shapes created by light displays were declined by the town a couple of years ago. That's more of a sport for those who enjoy creating light paintings.

"Care to clue me in, Mark?" I ask.

"No," he says, then claps his hands. "This will be great."

I look around us to see if I missed something but come out empty. We're the only ones on the street.

"What?" I step back.

"Go home and make your special Hot Chocolate. Then meet me with the hot chocolate behind Ricky's bar."

Excitement and anticipation fill his voice. The energy is contagious as an eagerness comes over me.

"And you won't tell me what we're doing until I meet you there?" I ask him to make sure.

"Exactly." He nods.

"Call it a deal. I'll see you in an hour behind Ricky's."

Before I can step back, Mark pulls me forward and our lips seal. All I can smell is wood and pine. My only thought is how right the world feels right now. It's over way too soon. In the next moment, he steps back and I'm left there breathless.

"See you there in an hour," he says over his shoulder as he turns the corner at the end of the street into the alleyway.

"Alright," I say, but he is gone and I'm left standing there breathless and hopeful.

When he says we got this, I believe him.

Chapter Eight

Ross is not thrilled to see me knocking at his door. But after I explain my plans, he has no choice but to let me in his store after hours. He's upset he didn't think of my idea first, but it's gracious enough to help me get the items I need.

"It's almost like I'm part of it," he says as he locks the door behind him.

"Almost," I say.

Part of the fun of the traditions is having the town guess who's behind it. It all gets revealed in the end, but the less I say the better.

He gives me a wink. "Get those lights to Rosa and help her complete her addition. Next year, I will acquire both of you to help me."

"If she's here next year."

I don't mean to say it out loud, but it slips out. Knowing that time with Rosa is limited hurts. I hate that I don't know where her head is or that she's one decision away from drifting again.

Ross looks down at the bags in my hands. "I have a

feeling she's looking for something to ground her and she might've found it in Maples."

"I think you're right," I say.

Her dream of adding a tradition might just do the trick. Maybe after this she'll have something to come back to and I'll be here waiting when she does.

"Say that again with Patty around and we're even." Ross claps his hands.

My smile is wide as I say, "You got a deal!"

"One last thing, Mark. Can you type the name of whatever you're planning on using to keep the lights on overnight?"

I take his phone and see the internet browser is already open. I type the name and style of battery I have and hand it back to him. With one last farewell, Ross goes his own way. Perhaps he wants to be ahead of the crowd and have his own on the way.

I make one last stop at home for a very important addition to tonight's plan. The lights cannot stay on without an electricity source. So they will need a little help from my solar battery pack. By the time I round the corner behind Ricky's bar, big fluffy flakes begin to fall.

Rosa is under the only light post, shivering lightly. She spots me at the same time I see her. Our eyes lock across the parking lot and mirroring smiles paint our faces.

"I hope you haven't been waiting long," I say.

She hands me a cup and pockets that hand to the warmth of her jacket. She's wearing a light pink hat and a matching scarf. They both glow almost white in this light, with the snow all around.

"What do you have there?" She looks over at the backpack on my back.

I tap it with my empty hand. "Everything we need is right here."

"So where to next?" she asks.

I point back towards the open forest behind Ricky's bar. Rosa follows my gaze and faces the open field.

"Let's go deep enough that we're out of sight, but not too deep where people can't see the tree light up from the street."

"What?" She looks at me over her shoulder.

"Our tradition will be decorating a small tree with lights out in the open."

I open my arms and gesture at our canvas.

"How will we keep the lights on?" she asks.

I pull my backpack forward and unzip it. I pull my small solar pack I purchased intending to charge my phone while camping. Rosa's eyes light up with excitement at the sight of the solar power.

"Will it charge during the day to keep the lights on the next day?"

I nod. I've no idea how many days it'll do it for as some winter days have close to no sun out, but it's fully packed right now and the lights Ross sold me won't take much power to light up.

"You know what this means?" Rosa lends closer to me.

My skin sparks to life.

"What?" I nearly shutter.

"We've got a tree to find and a town to shock come morning time."

Rosa takes my hand in hers and leads me into the woods. We go from tree to tree looking for just the right one. We have four boxes of lights at hand so the tree cannot be too big or too small that it won't be noticed.

Once we find the perfect tree, we test the lights and begin our tradition.

"Let me take a photo of you," I say and snap a quick shot.

Rosa does the final round of the lights and plugs them into the power source. The tree lights up in soft colorful lights.

"Let's do one with my phone, too." Rosa pads her pants, then jacket. "My phone isn't here." She looks around on the ground. "You think I could've dropped it?"

"You texted me when you left, right?" I look around with my flashlight.

"I had it in the parking lot for sure." She gestures toward Ricky's parking lot.

"Wait." I toss everything inside my backpack and stash it under the light-up tree. "We can come back for this."

The fresh snow covering the ground makes it difficult to see anything as we walk through Ricky's parking lot.

"Let's retrace your steps," I suggest, motioning for her to lead the way back.

Chapter Nine

Blue and red lights reflect off the snow all around us. Sheriff Johnny steps out of his car and points a flashlight in our eyes. The light is so bright I'm partly disoriented by the intrusion.

"What are you doing here?" He barks at us.

Here we go. Not even an hour before we're outed for our deed. It's not bad or illegal, but I was hoping to hear whispers in town of who could've been behind it first. In the minutes it took us to do it, I daydreamed of how it would all come to be. This is not what I hoped for.

Mark steps in front of me, shielding me from the light. "We're out for a walk."

Johnny finally lowers the flashlight from our eyes. "Sure you were," he says. His glare has an underline of cockiness. "There have been no homes attacked tonight."

"That's great," Mark and I say in unison.

"Yet," Johnny finishes. "I think if I keep my eyes on you two, those houses won't be hit."

"You gotta be kidding me," Mark says in a serious tone.

"If you have nothing to hide, then come with me." Johnny shrugs.

"To jail?" I gasp.

"We have no plans to vandalize anything. We're actually on our way home." Mark is trying to hold back his temper, but I can feel it on the edge.

"Will you finally leave us alone if we go with you?" I ask Johnny.

Mark rounds on me. "Don't give him what he wants. He doesn't have enough to arrest us."

"Well, I know that, but we only have to stay until whoever is doing this commits tonight's crime. We won't be there all night."

Mark doesn't look convinced, but he nods. What a memorable way to end the night.

I walk over to Johnny's car. "Open the door because we walked here and can't follow you to the station."

The sheriff looks a bit confused at the lack of transportation. If we were moving Christmas decorations from home to home, we would need a way to move stuff, but he's far too stubborn to give up now.

"Are you sure about this?" Mark asks me as we close the cop car door behind us.

I lean my head back on the headrest. "Nope," I say. I interlock my fingers with his. "But we'll be alright."

I lose track of time inside the holding cell.

"Johnny, will you please let these kids out already?"

Patty's voice carries through the hall into the cell at the back of the police station.

"They're suspects, Grams." Johnny's voice is low.

"Grams?" Mark and I say at the same time.

How did I never put two and two together? As the echo of our voices carries, footsteps follow. Johnny and Patty join us. Both of them standing on the other side of the holding cells.

"Are you two related?" I ask Patty.

She shrugs. "My niece is his mother."

"The only grandmother I ever known." Johnny takes a seat behind a desk. "Like I told her. You two will be here till I know you're not the ones behind the vandalism."

"That's not how the law works!" a voice calls from the doorway.

"You tell him dear!" Patty claps.

Like a knight in shining armor, Cathy arrives with Romo in tow. Her hair is wild and her clothes are dirty. She has definitely been out all night.

"Well, you're alive." Romo shoots Mark and me a glare. "We've been up looking for you all night."

"We've been right here." Mark rolls his head, letting his forehead touch the metal bars.

"Well, your phone was behind Ricky's bar. I thought someone had kidnapped you. I almost called the police until I remembered how useless the force is, so I went with the next best thing." She points over at Romo, who somehow doesn't look at Cathy with the same glare he has for everyone else in the room.

"Hey!" Johnny stands up and rounds the desk to glare at Cathy. "I do my job right."

"You can't hold people without a reason." She crosses her arms and glares right back at him.

Romo stands between them with his hands up. "How long will they be here?"

"As soon as I know for sure, they aren't the ones vandalizing my town." Johnny sneers in our direction.

"You're so annoying!" Cathy yells towards the ceiling.

After a few more back and forth between Johnny and Cathy, a second policeman walks in. He looks around, trying to piece together what's happening.

"Hey Mark," he says and waves. "You got yourself in a pickle?"

"Hey Peter." Mark waves back and just rolls his head at the question.

"What's happening here?" Peter directs his question to Johnny.

"These two are being held until I know they aren't the ones behind the vandalism to the Christmas home decorations," Johnny explains with exasperation.

Peter scratches his head. "A report on the radio said that Lincoln called this morning and said Tommy's boys were caught on a doorbell camera. He called Patty first, knowing she would be quicker at coming here than the operators passing reports."

We all turn to the quiet woman sitting on a chair on the side of the room. She grins as the collective faces turn in her direction.

"You knew this since you arrived?" the sheriff asks her.

Patty nods with a soft smile. "I was planning on telling you, but everyone showed up and the plot thickened in the best of ways. You know how much I love a showdown."

Johnny looks close to hanging his head. He makes quick work of unlocking the doors and gesturing for us to get going.

Once outside, Mark and I look around for any sign that anyone knows what's standing out there in the forest.

Other than the usual commotion of morning Christmas activities, nothing looks out of the ordinary. Until we see the first cluster of kids whispering enthusiastically.

"What were you two doing out there, anyway?" Cathy asks us.

Mark and I don't answer as we watch as the group of kids run across the street into the light store. As one group enters another exit with a bundle of boxes in their hands.

"Could it?" Mark whispers in my ear.

I look at my wristwatch. It's already past ten in the morning. Enough time has passed that the word could've spread. There's a larger than usual crowd inside Ross' store for this time in the morning.

"Let's go see what the fuss is in Ross' store." Mark takes my hand in his and leads the way.

Cathy and Romo follow us with confused expressions.

"I was the first to see the tree light up out in the forest from my second-floor window. I knew what it was and got ahead of the game. The orders of small solar battery packs will be here by noon. If you wish to hold one, you'll have to pay for it in advance," Ross says to the crowd.

"The man is a business genius." Mark looks at Ross in awe.

Patty shakes her head. "You're giving that opportunist too much credit."

I laugh and look around at the craziness that Maples is. This place is like nothing else. How did I ever think I would ever get bored with this place?

"What are you laughing at?" Mark asks me as he leans over me.

"At how much I love this crazy town." I lean closer to him and press my lips to his. "I think it's time to look at long-term rentals."

He leans back just enough to look me in the eye. His own shine with so much wonder and perhaps fear of hoping.

"What?" The word is so soft.

"I guess I can ask Cathy if she'll let me move in," I say.

"I would love to have you!" she yells from somewhere behind me.

"Are you sure the drifter can finally settle?" Mark asks me.

"Vacations will always be an option. But coming home to Maples will always sound better than anything else. After all, soon enough everyone will know we're the ones behind the tree lights and we'll become legends."

Mark gestures to a few people who are eyeing us suspiciously. "If you keep looking so smug, they'll know for sure it was us."

I wrap my arms around his neck and pull him down to my level. "Maybe I'm smug about something else."

Our lips touch and, like every romance book I ever read, the world fades away. I've always read those lines as happy endings. For me, it's a beautiful beginning.

The End.

Acknowledgments

Another one done! I want to say a very special thank you to Sarelie, who always helps me read and edits my books diligently. You're a great friend. I know how much time and effort you put into it and I really appreciate it.

Daniel, my fiance and best friend. This wouldn't be nearly as fun if it wasn't for you.

This book was incredibly fun to write. I can see myself coming back to the town of Maples, Maine, for future stories. We will see :)

About The Author

Diana Denisse is a writer of high fantasy novels and avid romance book reader who puts the magical world living in her head onto paper. She spends her free time hiking and exploring national parks across the country, seeking the magic at our fingertips.

To learn more about future books, please follow the social media links below.

- instagram.com/AuthorDianaDenisse
- tiktok.com/@AuthorDianadenisse
- amazon.com/stores/author/B0D8WQSNVH/about

Made in the USA
Columbia, SC
06 January 2025